PRIDE AND PREJUDICE

JANE AUSTEN

PLAYMORE PUBLISHERS

Editor: Heather Hammonds
Cover Illustration: Terry Riley
Illustrations: Gilly Marklew
Typesetting: Midland Typesetters

Pride and Prejudice
First published in 2008 by
Playmore Inc., Publishers,
58 Main Street, Hackensack, N.J. 07601

Printed in China.

The Author
Jane Austen
(1775–1817)

Jane Austen was born in the village of Steventon, Hampshire, in England. Her father was a church minister and she was one of eight children. In 1795 the young Jane started work on a novel called *First Impressions*. Her father mailed the story to a publisher but it was sent back by return post, almost certainly unread.

It was one of the greatest publishing misjudgments of all time. The book, slightly rewritten and under a new title, *Pride and Prejudice*, was published seventeen years later. It was Austen's masterpiece and became one of the biggest bestsellers in history.

Austen started writing as a teenager. Her other great novels include *Sense and Sensibility*, *Mansfield Park*, *Emma*, *Persuasion*, and *Northanger Abbey*.

Contents

The Title

There are many different meanings of the words *pride* and *prejudice,* but Jane Austen uses them in the following sense:

Pride … having a high opinion of one's self-importance.

Prejudice … a too-hastily formed opinion of someone else.

The Main Characters
The Bennet Family

Mr. and Mrs. Bennet … the long-suffering father and the loving but hysterical mother of the five unmarried Bennet girls. The family live at Longbourn, in Hertfordshire, England.
Jane … the eldest girl, who sees the good in everyone.
Elizabeth … the free-spirited, witty, and intelligent heroine of the story.
Mary … the third daughter; a shy, serious girl.
Kitty and Lydia … the wild, selfish, and irresponsible younger sisters.
Mr. and Mrs. Gardiner … the uncle and aunt of the Bennet girls. They live in London.

The Bingley Family

Charles Bingley ... the handsome young bachelor who rents Netherfield, the estate next door to the Bennet family.

Caroline Bingley ... Mr. Bingley's spiteful and jealous sister.

The Darcy Family

Fitzwilliam Darcy ... Mr. Bingley's aristocratic and wealthy young bachelor friend. He owns the great Pemberley Estate.

Georgina Darcy ... Mr. Darcy's young sister.

Lady Catherine de Bourgh ... Mr. Darcy's domineering and arrogant aunt who lives with her heiress daughter at Hunsford Park in Kent.

And...

The Reverend William Collins ... A cousin of Mr. Bennet, he is Lady de Bourgh's pompous church minister.

George Wickham ... A roguish military man whose father used to be steward at Pemberley Estate.

Chapter 1
The Five Bennet Girls

Mrs. Bennet loved her five daughters, who all still lived at home. Yet, she would have given anything to see two or three of them scattered around the countryside, married to wealthy aristocratic gentlemen, and living in large stately homes.

Mrs. Bennet posed as someone slightly more wealthy and aristocratic than she truly was. And she saw it as her role in life to marry off her daughters, Jane, Elizabeth, Mary, Kitty, and Lydia.

A nervous and hysterical woman, she thought that whenever a young man with a fortune came knocking on her door, then he must be looking for a wife. And news had just reached her that a Mr. Bingley, both wealthy and single, was coming to live on the neighboring property of Netherfield.

"A single man with a large fortune, they say," Mrs. Bennet said to her husband. "What good news!"

A nervous and hysterical woman.

"Why good news, my dear?" replied the long-suffering Mr. Bennet, who already knew the answer to his question, but liked to humor his wife regarding his five daughters.

"Don't be foolish," snapped Mrs. Bennet. "If the man is single and young, then there's every chance he will fall in love with one of our daughters."

Mr. Bennet also loved his five daughters, despite some of their undoubted imperfections. He loved his dear and equally imperfect wife, too. However, a man who shared his house with five daughters and a wife needed to make regular escapes to the peace and quiet of his study. And that's where he was to be found on most days.

One afternoon, Mr. Bennet was hiding in his study when there was a knock at the door.

"Can I come in, Papa?" asked a soft voice. It was his eldest daughter, Jane. She didn't wait for an answer but came straight in. "Papa," she said. "We've all heard about Mr. Bingley. When can we visit him?"

"Your dear mother has already asked me the same question," said Mr. Bennet, patiently. "You'll have to wait for an invitation."

"But you'll visit him to introduce yourself,

5

won't you, Papa?" cried Jane.

Mr. Bennet refused to say whether he would or wouldn't. He teased his daughters a great deal.

The truth was that Mr. Bennet had always intended to visit his new neighbors on his own, at the first opportunity. His first visit was meant to be a secret. But he was spotted by his girls, walking back across the fields from Netherfield.

Mr. Bennet was quickly surrounded.

"What's he like?" cried Jane.

"Is he good-looking?" asked Mary.

"Does he wear fashionable clothes?" asked Kitty.

"I expect he'll be far too old for me," said Lydia, the youngest, at fifteen, yet the tallest of the Bennet brood.

Elizabeth, the most down-to-earth of the Bennet girls, didn't seem that interested. She watched, smiling, as her sisters interrogated their father. But he was giving no answers.

Just then, Mrs. Bennet appeared. "My nerves are all a-twitter," she blustered. "I know where you've been. You must tell us everything."

"Your nerves, Mrs. Bennet," he replied, "have been in a twitter ever since I married you

"Is he good-looking?"

twenty years ago. Your nerves are old friends to me now."

"Mr. Bennet!" protested his wife, who never called her husband anything other than Mr. Bennet. "Stop making fun of me. We are all dying to hear your news."

Mr. Bennet took a deep breath and smiled. "I am not going to tell you anything," he said. "You'll find out about Mr. Bingley all in good time. He's coming to the monthly ball on Saturday week, with his sister Caroline and a Mr. Fitzwilliam Darcy."

The monthly ball was held in the nearby market town of Meryton. It was the major social event of the month for all the families in the area.

"Can we go, Papa?" asked young Lydia.

Everyone waited for Mr. Bennet's answer. At last he spoke. "Yes, as long as you don't expect me to come too."

Mr. Bennet preferred the peace and quiet of his study. He preferred a good book to facing the dangers of the dance floor.

He looked at his wife. "Mrs. Bennet," he said, "perhaps you'll find a husband for one of our dear girls at the ball. That should stop at least some of your nerves a-twittering!"

At last, the evening of the ball arrived. Mrs. Bennet, her daughters, and Elizabeth's best friend Charlotte Lucas, made sure they were all there in time to see the Bingley party arrive.

Mr. Bingley came in with his sister Caroline, a spindly dark-haired young woman, dressed in the latest London fashions. They were with their friend Mr. Darcy, a young man about the same age as Mr. Bingley.

Mr. Bingley was a good-looking man with a gentle face. He looked every inch a gentleman, but it was Mr. Darcy who attracted the attention of everyone in the room.

Mr. Darcy was tall and even more handsome than Mr. Bingley. He had a noble air and walked into the room as though he owned it.

Indeed, rumor had it that Mr. Darcy was fabulously rich. He was a gentleman farmer, and owned the great English country estate of Pemberley.

Elizabeth Bennet took one glance at him and decided that he looked the proudest and most disagreeable man in the room!

Chapter 2
The Night of the Ball

Mr. Darcy caught the eyes of all the ladies at the ball. Yet, before long, they had all decided that he was rude, far too proud, and distinctly unfriendly.

Mr. Bingley had been dancing all night, but Mr. Darcy took to the ballroom floor just once—and that was with Mr. Bingley's sister, Caroline. He spent the rest of the evening walking around the room by himself, only occasionally stopping to talk to either Mr. Bingley or Caroline.

It was one of these conversations that Elizabeth Bennet overheard. She had been dancing for most of the evening and had sat down to rest. Mr. Darcy was close by and she clearly heard what was said between him and Mr. Bingley.

"Come, Darcy," said Mr. Bingley. "You must do more dancing. I hate seeing you standing by yourself all the time."

"I certainly won't," replied Mr. Darcy. "I do not like dancing with people I have never met before. Besides, apart from your sister, dancing with anyone here would be a punishment to me. I have no time for any of these country folk."

"You shouldn't be so fussy," said Mr. Bingley. "I have never met so many pleasant girls before. And some of them are extremely pretty. I have danced with Jane Bennet, and she is a delight."

"Apart from your sister," replied Mr. Darcy, "that Bennet girl is the only good-looking lady in the room."

"Yes, she is the most beautiful creature I have ever seen," said Mr. Bingley. "But, look behind you. Elizabeth Bennet is just as good-looking. Let me introduce you."

Mr. Darcy turned to glance at Elizabeth, who was looking away from the two men but still listening to their conversation. He held up his hand to stop Mr. Bingley from making an introduction.

"Some might say she has some sort of good looks," he said, "but she is not attractive enough to tempt me onto the dance floor. So, Bingley, it would be better if you returned to

11

your dance partner and stopped wasting your time with me."

Mr. Bingley followed his advice and walked off to join Jane on the dance floor again.

Elizabeth had clearly heard Mr. Darcy's insults. Her first reaction was to think how pompous and proud the man was.

The rest of the evening passed without incident. Mrs. Bennet was in a mood of high excitement, her nerves a-twittering as never before. After all, hadn't Mr. Bingley danced with Jane twice already? And wasn't he worth at least several thousand pounds a year?

They all returned to their home of Long-bourn in good spirits and found Mr. Bennet still up and reading a book.

"Oh! My dear Mr. Bennet!" cried Mrs. Bennet entering the room. "What a delightful evening we've all had. You should have been there."

Mr. Bennet put his book down with a quiet sigh as Mrs. Bennet burst into an excited report of everything that had happened at the ball.

"Mr. Bingley danced with Jane twice," she began. "No one else danced with him twice. Mr. Bingley thought her quite beautiful, I'm sure. Just think of it, my dear. He actually danced

She clearly heard what was said.

with her twice. Oh, he is so handsome. And his sister, so elegant! I never saw so much lace on a dress before."

Mrs. Bennet would have carried on forever about the delights of Mr. Bingley if her husband hadn't stopped her.

"Mrs. Bennet," he said wearily. "No more! You'll be telling me next he sprained his ankle from dancing too much but gallantly carried on despite the agony."

But Mrs. Bennet wasn't finished. "We saw Mr. Darcy too," she said. "Our Lizzie would do well to keep well clear of him. He is so conceited and arrogant! Lizzie tells me that he said she wasn't pretty enough to dance with."

Mr. Bennet patiently listened to the rest of his wife's gossip, while the girls crept off to bed.

Upstairs, Jane and Elizabeth talked long into the night.

"Mr. Bingley is just what a young man should be," said Jane. "He's good-looking, sensible, lively, and with a good sense of humor. And he has such perfect manners. But why he asked me to dance twice, I will never know."

"That's the difference between us," replied Elizabeth. "Compliments always take you by surprise. I don't know why you don't expect

Mr. Bingley joined Jane on the dance floor again.

men to like you. You were five times more attractive than any other woman in the room tonight."

Jane laughed. "Sweet Lizzie, you are too kind," she said.

"I wish I could be like you," said Elizabeth. "The entire world is good in your eyes. I never heard you speak ill of anyone in my life. What say you about Mr. Darcy?"

"I know what you overheard tonight," said Jane, "but I also know that Mr. Bingley likes him very much. So he can't be all bad."

Talking long into the night.

The Night of the Ball

That same night, all the talk at Netherfield was about the ball. Mr. Bingley said that he had never met a nicer group of ladies. Caroline, not given to making many compliments, remarked that Jane and Elizabeth looked rather pretty.

Mr. Darcy wasn't there to make any comment. He had gone to bed, glad that the evening's so-called entertainment was over. There was no trace of Elizabeth Bennet in his dreams that night.

Chapter 3
Pride and Prejudice

The next day, Elizabeth took the short walk across the fields to visit her friend, Charlotte. Miss Bennet and Miss Lucas had much to talk about following the ball.

Charlotte had also heard about how rude Mr. Darcy had been about the ball, and about Elizabeth in particular. "I don't understand it, Lizzie," she said. "Mr. Darcy is a fine young man. He comes from a distinguished family and has a fortune. Perhaps, he has a right to feel proud and look down on us country cousins."

"I don't think so," replied Elizabeth. "I can forgive him his pride. But, despite my laughing at it now, I can't forgive him for his unkind remarks about me and the people of this area."

"Perhaps it's a matter of his pride and your prejudice," smiled Charlotte, teasingly. "You think he's too proud. Yet, perhaps, you feel biased against him because he is used to

"I don't understand it, Lizzie."

spending his time with people of a different or higher social circle."

"I don't know about that," replied Elizabeth. "But you can be sure that I shall not be dancing with Mr. Darcy in future, even if he went down on bended knee to ask me!"

Charlotte changed the topic of conversation to Jane. "Mr. Bingley likes your sister very much," she said. "That is obvious. But will Jane ever let him know how welcome his affection is? She is not very confident in herself. If she doesn't encourage Mr. Bingley, he might lose interest and look elsewhere for a wife."

Elizabeth disagreed. "It is up to a man to find out if someone likes him. But love and marriage are matters of chance, and I like Mr. Bingley. So I shall do all I can to encourage Jane to pursue her interest in him."

***

So the days passed. Mr. Bingley became a regular caller at the Bennet residence. He was often accompanied by Mr. Darcy. The man still had a few more weeks to spend with his friend before returning to his Pemberley estate.

One afternoon, Mary, the most serious

Bennet girl, was playing some music for them on the piano. Charlotte was with them too, and she was in a playful mood. She saw that Darcy was once again standing by himself.

"There's nothing like dancing, Mr. Darcy," she said enthusiastically. "Why not take Elizabeth onto the floor. Surely, you could not refuse such an invitation?"

Mr. Darcy was forced to make a reply. "I do like dancing in the right social circles," he said, "but it's a sad reflection of our times that it has become fashionable in less polished societies. Every Tom, Dick, and Harry takes to the dance floor these days."

Elizabeth heard the words. "Charlotte," she said within earshot of Mr. Darcy, "I have no intention of dancing with Mr. Darcy. If I want to dance, I shall choose my own partner. And it definitely won't be Mr. Darcy!"

With that, she walked out of the room. No one said a word. Mary started playing the piano again to cover up the silence.

***

That evening at Netherfield, Caroline Bingley heard how Elizabeth had snubbed Mr. Darcy.

"I shall choose my own partner."

"How rude!" she exclaimed. "Has the woman no manners?"

"Perhaps I am too proud," replied Mr. Darcy. "Perhaps I am wrong in criticizing what I might call lesser country folk. Perhaps I should dance more, with more ordinary people."

Caroline was most surprised at his change in attitude. "And who has made you change your mind?" she asked.

"Miss Elizabeth Bennet," replied Mr. Darcy.

"Miss Elizabeth Bennet!" cried Caroline. "I am astonished. You didn't even dance with her at the ball. And you certainly haven't said a civil word to her since."

"A man can change his mind," replied Mr. Darcy.

"How long since this change of mind took place?" smiled Caroline, enjoying a joke at Mr. Darcy's expense. "Are we to expect a marriage sooner or later?"

"That is exactly the question I expected you to ask," replied Mr. Darcy. "Why is a lady's imagination so rapid? It jumps from admiration to love and from love to matrimony, in two quick leaps."

"But just think about it," continued

Caroline. "Marry a Bennet girl and you would gain that dreadful woman Mrs. Bennet as a mother-in-law."

Mr. Darcy took the joke in good humor, but recognized Caroline's bitter edge behind it. Caroline was a jealous woman at the best of times.

Mr. Darcy had ignored Elizabeth at the ball. He had often remarked to his friends at Netherfield that she had nothing to attract him. Yet, in a few brief seconds that afternoon, he had seen something special in her. In her cold rejection of him, he had seen her looks,

"Are we to expect a marriage?"

her strong character. The flash of anger in her darkly attractive eyes had disturbed him.

He might still argue that her manners and upbringing didn't belong to the high society of his more fashionable world. But there was something about her that he admired. He found his thoughts returning to her again and again . . .

Chapter 4
Jane is Invited to Netherfield

Kitty and Lydia, the youngest Bennet girls, had none of the concerns of their older sisters. As yet, finding a husband did not concern them. That was not to say that they didn't take plenty of notice of the most handsome young men in town.

Longbourn was only a mile away from the town of Meryton. The two girls regularly walked there to see what fun they could find. They were both rather scatterbrained, unlike their older sisters. Mr. Bennet fondly imagined that Kitty and Lydia's minds were completely empty of common sense.

The trouble with Lydia was that she was not only scatterbrained, but wild and disobedient too. She was particularly excited on hearing the news that the regional army militia had just set up its headquarters in Meryton. With England still at war with France, most towns had their own soldiers to guard against any invasion.

Lydia, with Kitty in tow as usual, lost no time in marching swiftly into town. There the girls attracted the attention of the most handsome soldiers. In no time at all, Kitty had met a Captain Carter and promised to love him forever. Lydia was much more of a flirt. She wasn't old enough to win the heart of an officer. But she had her favorites among the younger soldiers.

Mr. Bennet was horrified at the behavior of his two daughters. "I suspected they were two of the silliest girls in the county," he remarked to his wife one evening. "Now I am absolutely convinced they are."

"They are very clever girls at times," replied Mrs. Bennet. "Remember how young they are. At their age, you can't expect them to behave like their ageing parents. Besides, if a wealthy colonel in the army decided he wanted to marry one of my girls, I should not refuse him."

The argument was halted by the delivery of a note from Netherfield. It was from the Bingley family, inviting Jane to dinner.

"I must accept, Mother dear, mustn't I?" said Jane. "Can I take the carriage? It's going to rain, I'm sure."

"It isn't possible," replied Mrs. Bennet.

Marching swiftly into town.

"The carriage horses are needed on the farm just now, so you'll have to walk. You can stay the night if the rain is heavy."

So it was agreed. That afternoon, Jane set off alone. It began to rain soon after and by the time she got to Netherfield she was soaked through.

Late in the evening, a note from Jane arrived at Longbourn.

I got very wet on my way here and now I have a chill. My kind friends will not let me out into the cold and I am to stay at Netherfield until I recover. Do not worry; I am in very good hands.
. All my love,
Jane

The next day was cloudy and cold, but Elizabeth decided to walk over to Netherfield to see Jane. She was very worried about her sister. As she set off, the rain began to fall once more.

Elizabeth started to run, jumping over gates and springing over puddles. She was really enjoying herself. She was not the least concerned that she reached Netherfield covered in mud and with a red face from the exercise.

Jane was soaked through.

She was shown into the parlor. Mr. Bingley was quite astounded that Elizabeth had come the whole way on foot in such bad weather. But he greeted her with a warm smile. Mr. Darcy was there too, and he just nodded. Caroline shook Elizabeth's hand without much affection at all, but she took her away to find some dry clothes.

It seemed that Jane was sicker than they had thought. She hadn't slept and she had a fever. She wasn't well enough to leave her room. After Elizabeth had changed into some dry clothes, she was taken to see her.

Jane was exhausted but was pleased to see her younger sister. "I shall quickly recover," she sniffed. "I'll be home soon."

Mr. Bingley spotted that Elizabeth was reluctant to leave her sister. So he said she could stay at Netherfield until Jane was better. Mr. Bingley was most concerned about Jane's health. He gave her every care and attention.

Elizabeth gratefully accepted the invitation and a servant was dispatched to Longbourn to give the Bennet family the news and also bring back some more clothes for Elizabeth.

Chapter 5
Elizabeth and Jane at Netherfield

Elizabeth spent that first evening with Jane in an upstairs bedroom. Meanwhile, downstairs, Caroline was talking with Mr. Darcy and Mr. Bingley.

"Miss Elizabeth Bennet has nothing to recommend her," said Caroline, "except her ability to walk three miles. I shall never forget her appearance when she arrived. She looked like a muddy scarecrow. Why on earth did she come? Why did she scamper across the country just because Jane has a harmless cold?"

Mr. Bingley did his best to defend Elizabeth. "Her coming shows a great affection for her sister," he said.

But Caroline immediately sought the support of Mr. Darcy. "Mr. Darcy," she said, "I am sure you would not approve if your sister made such a fool of herself by running across the muddy fields."

Mr. Bingley did his best to defend Elizabeth.

Mr. Darcy agreed, a little half-heartedly.

"Dear brother," continued Caroline, "I hope this display of a lack of social skills in Elizabeth will make you think twice about your strange affection for Jane. She is undoubtedly a pea from the same pod."

"Be quiet, sister!" replied Mr. Bingley. "I shall do no such thing. I have a great regard for Miss Jane Bennet."

"But the Bennets have no money," protested Caroline.

"If they only had one penny," said Mr. Bingley, "that would make no difference to how much I liked her."

Elizabeth came down later to find everyone playing a game of cards. Mr. Bingley asked if she wanted to join in the game. She declined. "Thank you for asking me," she said politely, "but I would rather read a book,"

"You would rather read a book, would you?" scoffed Caroline. "What a strange choice."

Mr. Bingley saw the way the conversation was going and interrupted and pointed to the bookshelves. "Take your pick," he said.

Elizabeth thanked Mr. Bingley and went over to choose a book.

Once more Caroline had something to say.

"You have such a small collection of books, dear brother," she said. "But I'm sure you have seen Mr. Darcy's collection at Pemberley. No one has a better library than Mr. Darcy."

The next morning Elizabeth sent a note to Longbourn, asking her mother to visit.

Mrs. Bennet would never refuse the chance to visit Netherfield. She had no idea that Caroline Bingley thought her socially inferior to them and dreaded the thought of her visiting.

Mrs. Bennet arrived just after the doctor had visited Jane. He had ordered that Jane should stay in bed. "I'm afraid my family must trespass on your hospitality for a little longer," she said. "Jane can't leave her bed yet."

"Trespass!" exclaimed Mr. Bingley. "Jane can stay here as long as is needed. I'm sure my sister wouldn't hear of her being sent home yet."

"Of course not," said Caroline, coldly. "Jane will receive every care while she is with us."

"You are so kind, Miss Bingley," said Mrs. Bennet. "I'm sure I don't know what would become of us without having such good friends as you. You are the finest country folk I know."

Mr. Darcy interrupted at that moment.

"Madam, I don't see myself as a country bumpkin."

"Oh, I would never suggest such a thing," said Mrs. Bennet, apologetically. "All I meant was that our social lives are just as busy and interesting in the country, as people who live in the fashionable areas of London. I cannot see that London has any advantages over the country. The country is a far pleasanter place."

"I would have to disagree," said Darcy.

Elizabeth saw that her mother was about to cause a huge argument. So she interrupted the conversation. "Mama," she said, "Mr. Darcy only means that you are more likely to meet a wider mix of people in town. And that has to be true."

Mrs. Bennet was saved from saying anything more embarrassing by Elizabeth asking Mr. Bingley a question. "You promised to hold a ball at Netherfield. Have you set a date yet?"

Mrs. Bennet was horrified at her daughter's forwardness. "Miss Elizabeth Bennet!" she gasped. "Don't be so rude."

"No. No," said Mr. Bingley. "Elizabeth is right. I did say I would hold a ball here. And as she has caught me out, I give her my full permission to set the date and I will organize it."

"I don't see myself as a country bumpkin."

Now it was Caroline's turn to be horrified. The thought of the dreadful Bennet mother coming to a ball at Netherfield was almost too much to bear.

***

In the days that followed, Mr. Darcy became increasingly irritated at the attention given to him by Caroline Bingley. Was the woman falling in love with him?

One morning, Caroline found Mr. Darcy writing a letter to his young sister, Georgiana Darcy. "How delighted Miss Darcy will be to receive a letter from you," she gushed.

Mr. Darcy ignored the comment and continued writing.

"You write very quickly," observed Caroline, still trying to catch his attention.

"You are mistaken," he said at last. "I write rather slowly."

"Please tell your sister how I long to see her," continued Caroline.

"I have already," said an increasingly irritated Mr. Darcy, whose pen had started to scratch rather badly.

"Oh, let me mend your pen," begged

Trying to catch his attention.

Caroline. "I am awfully good at mending pens."

"Thank you," said Mr. Darcy, "but I always mend my own."

"And do tell your sister how delighted I am that she is learning to play the harp."

"I will," snapped Mr. Darcy.

"Do you always write such long letters?" asked Caroline.

"Only when you ask me to tell my sister so many things!"

Mr. Darcy was relieved when Caroline finally left him alone and went off to do some needlework.

***

In the evening, Mr. Bingley played the piano while Elizabeth and Caroline sang.

A little later, Elizabeth could not help noticing how often Mr. Darcy fixed his eyes on her. Then she was shocked to see him rise and approach her.

"Miss Bennet," he said, "would you like to dance?"

Elizabeth smiled but made no answer. Mr. Darcy repeated the question.

"I heard you the first time," said Elizabeth, mischievously, "but I wasn't sure how to reply. You might accuse me of being unfashionable in the way I dance. You had no wish to dance with me before."

For the first time, Mr. Darcy knew that she had overheard his remark at the Meryton Ball.

"So I think," continued Elizabeth, "that the answer to your question is no."

Mr. Darcy was speechless.

Caroline Bingley was livid. She had heard the conversation and was suddenly very jealous. Elizabeth was now becoming a rival to her over the matter of Mr. Darcy's attentions.

Later that same evening when Elizabeth had retired, Caroline asked her brother if he really was going to have a ball at Netherfield.

"Of course," he said. "I gave Miss Elizabeth Bennet my word."

"You do realize," she replied, "that there are some among us who would consider this ball a punishment rather than a pleasure. Some of us more used to society balls will quickly tire of some of the country folk who might attend *your* ball. It just won't do!"

Chapter 6
A Very Pompous Man

The main reason Mrs. Bennet desperately wanted to see one or more of her daughters married to someone rich lay in the family's constant state of poverty. The Bennets were, in society terms, the most important residents of the village of Longbourn. But they didn't have the income to match their social position.

The other reason was that the house they lived in was the subject of an old family legal agreement. It demanded that the nearest male relative to the family should inherit the property.

There being no boys in the Bennet family, the law was quite clear in what should happen. When Mr. Bennet died, the Longbourn house would become the property of his cousin, the Reverend William Collins.

Mr. Collins had just become the minister of the church in the village of Hunsford, in Kent. He had only been given the job at the request of the village's most important resident, Lady Catherine de Bourgh.

Soon after Jane's complete recovery and her return to Longbourn, Mr. Bennet announced to the family that he had received a letter from the Reverend Collins.

"In case you are not aware of it," Mr. Bennet said, "he is the man who, when I am dead, can turn you all out of this house as soon as it pleases him."

"Oh dear! Oh dear!" cried Mrs. Bennet. "I cannot bear the thought; to be thrown out in the street without money or a roof over our heads!"

Mr. Bennet tried to calm his wife. "The letter I have received may make you a little happier," he replied. "Then again, it might do the opposite."

With that, he read out the rather pompous letter that the Reverend Collins had sent:

Dear Mr. Bennet,

I am well aware that the fact I shall inherit your house when you die has caused a rift between us. It is a rift I want to heal.

As you know, I have recently had the good

Mr. Bennet had received a letter.

fortune to be employed as minister to the Lady de Bourgh's church. Her bounty and generosity knows no bounds. I shall be indebted to her for the rest of my life.

In turn, I feel that I must promote God's work wherever I can. I do, of course, recall your lovely daughters. I think that I would be failing in my duty if I did not at least try to teach them the path of goodness. With that in mind, I wish to announce that I shall be at your door at four o'clock on Monday, November 18. I shall stay with you until the following Saturday. I must, of course, be back in my pulpit for Lady de Bourgh by the Sunday.

I remain your friend and well-wisher,
Reverend William Collins.

"There you are," said Mr. Bennet, folding up the letter. "So we may all expect our visitor on Monday."

"He sounds very pompous," said Mary, the Bennet's middle daughter.

"No more pompous than Lady de Bourgh, I'm sure," said Elizabeth sharply.

"Elizabeth!" said Mrs. Bennet. "That's no way to talk of such a distinguished lady."

45

***

The Reverend Collins duly arrived at exactly four o'clock on the eighteenth.

He was a short man of about twenty-five. His manners were very formal and he complemented the five Bennet girls as soon as they all sat down to supper.

"I had heard of their beauty," he remarked to Mrs. Bennet. "All I can say is that they are all more beautiful than I ever imagined. I'm sure they will all soon be married."

"Indeed, I hope so," said Mrs. Bennet. "If they are not well married, we will all be very poor indeed."

"Ah," said Mr. Collins. "I think you are referring to the matter of your house. I am well aware of the position my dear cousins could find themselves in. I think there may be a way around that problem. I cannot say anything just yet, but I might just stress that I do find your daughters very handsome indeed. And Lady de Bourgh has promised that she will allow me to marry when I find the right person."

During dinner, Mr. Bennet hardly said a word. But afterwards he had a talk with Mr. Collins. In truth, all he wanted to find out

46

A Very Pompous Man

The Reverend Collins arrives.

was whether the young man was as foolish as he seemed to be. "Tell me about Lady de Bourgh," he said. "She sounds a very kind person."

"Oh she is," said Mr. Collins. "Lady de Bourgh is absolutely charming. Her kindness knows no limits. Her looks mark her out as distinguished beyond measure. I count my blessings in being able to serve her. And, dare I say it, she treats me more like a friend than a loyal servant. She has twice asked me to dine. And she allows me to live in a small cottage just a few yards from the bottom of her garden."

Mr. Bennet tried to hide the smile than kept coming to his lips. He was enjoying every minute of the man's company. Mr. Collins truly was stupid and absurd.

Chapter 7
Mr. Collins's Marriage Plans

The next morning Mr. Collins went in search of a private moment with Mrs. Bennet.

"Mrs. Bennet," he said, "would it be true to say that none of your girls are as yet engaged or promised to anyone? I am thinking of your delightful Jane."

"Well," replied Mrs. Bennet, "it is possible that she might become engaged quite soon. She enjoys the company of Mr. Bingley very much."

Mr. Collins only had to change the name as he searched for a more hopeful answer. "Your middle daughter Mary, would she be engaged?"

"I doubt Mary would ever want to marry," replied Mrs. Bennet. "She is far too serious a girl to lose her heart to anyone."

Mr. Collins knew that Kitty and Lydia were still too young to marry. So Elizabeth was the only one left.

A private moment with Mrs. Bennet.

"Elizabeth is so charming," he said. "I expect she is already spoken for."

"Oh no!" she replied. "She is indeed very single."

"Well, perhaps . . ." Mr. Collins was temporarily silenced by a sudden attack of nerves. He took a deep breath and began again. "Perhaps, I might take her for a walk one day," he said at last. "A walk is always a good start on the road to marriage."

Mrs. Bennet could not imagine for a moment how Elizabeth would react. All she could think of was that a few weeks ago she had five daughters with no hopes of marriage. Now it seemed she might get both Jane and Elizabeth off her hands in very quick time!

As for Mr. Bennet, he had quickly tired of Mr. Collins's stupidity and now he just wanted the man to go home. Every time he escaped into his study, Mr. Collins would follow him and begin yet another endless speech about Lady de Bourgh's good qualities. So he was quite pleased when a certain Mr. Wickham called to present himself to the family.

Mr. Wickham was a dashing military man of great charm and good looks. He had met the Bennet tearaways, Kitty and Lydia, and they had invited him to Longbourn to meet their parents. It turned out that Mr. Wickham's father had worked as steward to Mr. Darcy's father at Pemberley.

Elizabeth was quite interested to find out what he knew of Mr. Darcy. "Don't be afraid to talk honestly," she said. "I have just spent several days with him and I must say that I find him a very disagreeable person."

Mr. Wickham presents himself to the family.

Mr. Wickham seemed to enjoy hearing that news. "I must be careful what I say," he said, "but I too cannot forgive him for his behavior. Mr. Darcy's father was a fine man. My father worked for him, of course. But his son is a very different matter. I find his behavior scandalous."

Elizabeth was absolutely intrigued. "Do go on, sir," she said.

"The elder Mr. Darcy was my godfather and he gave me a good job on the estate at Pemberley," Mr. Wickham began. "He said that the job was mine for life. But when he died and young Darcy took over the house, he immediately threw me out. He had someone else he wanted to give my job to.

"I explained that his father had given me the job for as long as I lived. But Mr. Darcy refused to believe me. I was thrown out and that's when I joined the army."

"That is dreadful," said a shocked Elizabeth. "How could he go against his father's wishes? He deserves to be publicly disgraced!"

"He will be one day," said Mr. Wickham. "But not by me. I can never expose him for what he is. I have too much respect for his late father."

"He deserves to be publicly disgraced!"

"And what do you know of his sister, Miss Georgiana Darcy?" asked Elizabeth.

"There is no difference between them," he said. "Their lives are guided by one thing . . . pride!"

"What surprises me," said Elizabeth, "is why such a nice man as Mr. Bingley would have Mr. Darcy as a friend."

"Mr. Darcy has great charm," replied Mr. Wickham. "He uses it when he wants something."

That evening, Mr. Wickham had another snippet of gossip for Elizabeth. "I see that Mr. Collins is staying with you," he began. "I expect you know he has been given the church living in Lady de Bourgh's village. But did you know that she is Mr. Darcy's aunt?"

Elizabeth was most surprised. "I certainly did not," she said.

The next day she related to Jane all that she had heard from Mr. Wickham.

"Mr. Darcy appears to have fooled all his friends," said Jane. She too could not understand why Mr. Bingley had befriended such a rogue.

The two girls decided not to mention a word about what they knew. If the facts became public, it would only embarrass Mr. Bingley.

A short time later, the Bennets were visited by Mr. Bingley. He had come with an invitation to the eagerly awaited Netherfield Ball.

Chapter 8
The Netherfield Ball

Elizabeth, being an intelligent student of human nature, had guessed the main reason for Mr. Collins's visit to Longbourn. Her suspicion was strengthened when he asked her to reserve the first two dances at the Netherfield Ball for him.

Was she to be carried away by Mr. Collins to be the mistress of Hunsford Parsonage?

Mrs. Bennet hinted to her daughter that she would have no objections to a marriage between her and Mr. Collins. Elizabeth dreaded the idea of a marriage to Mr. Collins, yet she had taken a small interest in the rather dashing Mr. Wickham.

One thing she had decided was that there was to be no talk of Mr. Wickham's criticism of the Darcy family at the Netherfield Ball. After all, Mr. Darcy was Mr. Bingley's friend.

The night of the ball finally arrived. Elizabeth was a little surprised to discover that Mr.

Wickham was not present, despite the fact that she knew for sure that he had been invited.

Oh, how she wished it had been Mr. Collins who hadn't turned up! He quickly sidled up to her for his two promised dances. He was an awful dancer; awkward, stiff, and forever stumbling on his thin little legs. He spent the entire two dances apologizing for his lack of skill on the dance floor.

Mr. Collins pursued Elizabeth for further dances, but she was rescued by an unlikely person. She suddenly found herself face-to-face with Mr. Darcy. Then, before she knew it, she had accepted his request for a dance and was on the dance floor immediately after.

For some time, neither said a word. Elizabeth finally broke the ice with a comment about how the guests seemed to be enjoying the dancing. "Indeed," was Mr. Darcy's single word in reply.

There was a further period of silence between them before Elizabeth's sense of humor got the better of her. "Mr. Darcy, it's your turn to say something," she began. "I talked of the dancing and now, I think, it is your duty to talk about the size of the room or the state of the weather outside."

The night of the ball finally arrived.

Mr. Darcy smiled. "I will talk about anything you would like me to talk about," he replied. "Do you always talk when you're dancing?"

"Sometimes," she answered. "It helps to fill in the time when one's racing around the dance floor with a man who is dancing just out of duty rather than enjoyment."

That silenced Mr. Darcy for a moment. Elizabeth was feeling very mischievous and dropped the news that she had met Mr. Wickham. But she didn't say anything about the conversation she'd had with the man.

"Oh, how nice for you," said Mr. Darcy, coldly. "His good looks and charm quickly win him friends. Yet, I am not certain that he is capable of keeping those friends."

"He seems to have been unlucky in losing your friendship," added Elizabeth.

Mr. Darcy made no answer and clearly wanted to change the subject.

"I have enjoyed my dance with you, Mr. Darcy," said Elizabeth, with a smile. "But I have to admit that I have heard so many different things about you, that your true character still puzzles me."

"I am well aware that people say different things about me," he admitted, "yet I would

Dancing with Mr. Darcy.

advise you against making a quick conclusion as to my character. Try to moderate any prejudice you may have about me. Who knows, I might change your mind and reveal myself as a pleasanter man that you imagine. It is possible you are prejudiced against me for no good reason."

The conversation ended there as the music stopped and Miss Caroline Bingley hurriedly came between Elizabeth and Mr. Darcy, a fiercely jealous look in her eye.

"Elizabeth," she cried, "I hear that you have been enchanted by one Mr. George Wickham. I must warn you immediately that he is not one for speaking the truth. He has cruelly ill-used the Darcy family. Don't believe a word he tells you."

"I can think for myself!" said Elizabeth sharply, before quietly slipping away. "I can make my own mind up about whom I like."

"I told you she was a rude girl, Mr. Darcy," said Caroline. "Keep well away from her."

Poor Elizabeth, in her haste to escape Caroline, bumped straight into Mr. Collins again.

"Miss Elizabeth!" he cried. "Oh, what a night! I have just made the most amazing discovery. There is, in this very room, a relation of my dear friend and supporter, Lady Catherine de Bourgh. I must go to him this very minute and apologize for not realizing he was a relative."

"Who is he?" asked Elizabeth.

"Why, the richest man in the room," he said. "Mr. Darcy, no less. He is her ladyship's nephew. Oh, how exciting! I am in the unique position of being able to tell him that as of the last time I spoke with his aunt, she was in good health."

"Oh, how exciting!"

"I'm sure," said Elizabeth, hiding her smile, "that Mr. Darcy will be thrilled to hear that."

Elizabeth watched Mr. Collins hurry across to Mr. Darcy. She was too far away to hear what was said, but she did recognize the shape of some of the words on Mr. Collins's lips.

There was a definite, "I apologize" and a "Vicar of Hunsford" here and there and almost certainly several references to "My dearest Lady de Bourgh."

There weren't many more words she could detect. But the next moment, she saw Mr. Darcy slip away into the crowd, leaving Mr. Collins talking to himself.

Meanwhile, Mrs. Bennet was circulating, and trying to join in conversations with the most high-born ladies at the ball. Like Mr. Collins, she could never quite understand why she continually found herself all alone.

The Bennets were the last to leave Netherfield that evening. How Caroline Bingley sighed with relief as the front door finally closed on Mrs. Bennet.

Chapter 9
Mr. Collins Proposes

The morning after the ball, Mr. Collins found Elizabeth with her mother in the drawing room.

"Mrs. Bennet," he announced. "I'm sure you know what my business is today. Could you leave Elizabeth and me alone for a while?"

"Of course!" exclaimed Mrs. Bennet.

So Elizabeth was left alone with her pursuer.

"Dear Miss Elizabeth," he began. "I'm sure you know my purpose. Almost as soon as I entered this house, I singled you out as the companion of my future life. But first let me state my reasons why I came to Longbourn to look for a wife."

Poor Elizabeth sighed and tried to hide the laughter that was building up inside her.

"First," he said, "it is right for a clergyman like me to marry. Second, I'm sure it will greatly add to my happiness; and thirdly the

Left alone with her pursuer.

good Lady Catherine de Bourgh tells me I should marry. And she told me that I should choose someone who was clean, useful, and had the skills to make a very small annual income go a long way. And most importantly, if I did find someone, then I must present her to Lady de Bourgh to see if she approves."

Elizabeth might have been very angry at the last point, if she wasn't almost in fits of laughter at Mr. Collins's idea of a good wife.

"Now," continued Mr. Collins, "as you probably know, when your father dies, I inherit the house. It seemed obvious to me that I should choose one of his daughters. At least that way, the whole family won't have to look for a new home when I move in. And of course, I wouldn't object if they visited us occasionally. Now, nothing remains for me to do but to assure you of my affection toward you."

"You are too hasty, sir," said Elizabeth. "I thank you for the proposal, but it is impossible for me to accept. I'm afraid I must decline."

Mr. Collins just smiled. "I am well aware that it is usual for young ladies to reject the first proposal of marriage while always meaning to accept it in the end. So, my dear Elizabeth, rest assured that I am not disappointed. I still expect to lead you to the altar soon."

"Upon my word, Mr. Collins!" said Elizabeth, raising her voice for the first time. "Your expectations are extraordinary after what I have just said. I assure you that I am not one of those young ladies you talk about. I am perfectly serious in my refusal. You could never make me happy, and I am convinced that I am the last woman in the world to make you happy. I'm sure Lady de Bourgh would agree with me."

"Upon my word, Mr Collins!"

Mr. Collins was quite shaken by the firmness of Elizabeth's reply. "I cannot imagine that Her Ladyship would disapprove of my choice. And when I see her next I shall speak to her in the highest terms of your modesty, your expertise in domestic matters, and great common sense."

"Indeed, Mr. Collins," replied Elizabeth. "All praise will be unnecessary. I wish you all happiness in life. And by refusing you my hand, believe me, sir, I am doing all in my power to guarantee your happiness. And do take possession of the family's estate as soon as my father dies. I'm sure we will all be happy to move out at your will."

With that, Elizabeth made for the door and escape.

"When I have the honor of speaking to you next," he said, "I shall look forward to receiving a more favorable answer. I know a woman's mind. No sensible woman could refuse me. With Lady de Bourgh's support, I shall go far. So I must conclude that your rejection is only temporary."

Elizabeth sighed again. "I cannot speak plainer," she said. "I cannot and will not marry you."

With that, she left the room.

When Mrs. Bennet heard the news, she was completely flustered. "She cannot refuse you," she gasped. "I promise you, Mr. Collins, that she shall see good sense. She is a headstrong girl. But I will make her change her mind."

Mrs. Bennet went straight to her husband, who was quietly reading in his study.

"You must come and make Lizzie marry Mr. Collins!" she shrieked.

Mr. Bennet lowered his book and politely asked his wife what she expected him to do.

"Just tell her she must marry him!" she cried.

"I cannot do that," he said, "but I will speak with her."

Elizabeth was summoned to the study. "Is this true, Lizzie?" asked Mr. Bennet. "Have you refused Mr. Collins?"

"Yes, Papa."

"But your mother insists on you accepting him as a husband. Is that not so Mrs. Bennet?"

"Yes," she replied, "or I will never see or talk to Elizabeth again."

Mr. Bennet sighed. "Well, Elizabeth," he said, with a mischievous look, "you have a choice to make. It seems you are about to lose

"Just tell her she must marry him!"

one of your parents. Your mother has said that she will never see you again if you do not marry Mr. Collins. And for sure, I will never see you again if you do marry the idiot."

Elizabeth could do nothing but smile with relief that at least her father supported her.

Chapter 10
A Surprise Engagement

Mr. Collins never did come to accept Elizabeth's refusal. But one day he went out for a walk and wasn't seen again until late in the afternoon.

On his return, he went straight to see Mrs. Bennet. "I am to marry," he announced abruptly.

"Oh, thank goodness," sighed Mrs. Bennet. "Elizabeth has seen sense."

"No, it is not Elizabeth," he said. "I am to marry Miss Charlotte Lucas. I have her promise. I proposed this afternoon and she has accepted."

When Elizabeth heard the news she was shocked. What had possessed her best friend to agree to marry the man?

Jane was astounded too. "How extraordinary," she said. "A man with nothing to recommend him at all, asks two women to marry within a few days. And one of them accepts him!"

The truth was that the Lucas family had fallen on hard times financially. When they heard that Mr. Collins was in the employ of Lady de Bourgh and had good hopes for the future, they strongly advised Charlotte to accept him.

They had also made a quick calculation of how many more years Mr. Bennet might live; the answer told them how long it would be before the happy couple could take over the Longbourn property.

Elizabeth spoke with her friend later that day. "I know it surprises you, Lizzie," said Charlotte, "but I am not like you. I am not as pretty as you, nor as charming. I am already twenty-seven and I might never have the chance to marry again."

Elizabeth hated the idea of her friend throwing her life away by marrying someone who could never make her happy.

Mrs. Bennet was furious, of course. She could hardly bear to talk to Charlotte any more. She was still convinced that Elizabeth would have agreed to marry Mr. Collins eventually.

Now, all she could think of was two things. First, she had lost the chance to marry off one

"I know it surprises you, Lizzie."

of her daughters. Secondly, Charlotte would be the mistress of Longbourn when Mr. Bennet died.

Worse news was to follow the next day. Mr. Bingley had left to do some business in London and a letter arrived from Caroline Bingley.

Dear Mrs. Bennet,

By the time this reaches you, we will all have left for London. I feel sure that none of us will be back this winter. Most of our best friends have already returned to London, too. The countryside doesn't suit us in winter. I know Mr. Bingley feels the same.

Mr. Darcy will be with us in London and so will Georgiana, his lovely sister. There is no more beautiful a girl on earth. My brother Mr. Bingley has long admired her. We are sure they will marry. They are so suited.

Yours,
Caroline Bingley

The letter was handed around in silence to each member of the Bennet family. They all saw Jane's sad face, as she read it.

They all saw Jane's sad face.

"What does it mean?" she asked, putting down the letter.

"Dear sister," said Elizabeth putting her arm around Jane. "It is cruelly clear. Miss Bingley sees that her brother is in love with you, but she wants him to marry Miss Darcy. No doubt she has gone to London to persuade Mr. Bingley to stay there and forget all about you."

Jane could not believe anyone could be so cruel.

"We are not rich enough for Miss Bingley," continued Elizabeth. "We are not grand enough. Yes, we are useful as country playthings, but nothing more. She wants Miss Darcy for her brother. But I for one am sure of Mr. Bingley's true feelings for you."

"I cannot believe Caroline could be so deceiving," said Jane.

"Mr. Bingley is a man of strong independence," replied Elizabeth. "He will return before the winter is out."

At that time the only piece of good news for the Bennets was the departure of Mr. Collins for his home. His place was taken by Mr. Wickham, who became a regular visitor to Longbourn. In the absence of Mr. Darcy and

Mr. Bingley, gossip about Mr. Darcy's unfair treatment of Mr. Wickham spread like wildfire.

Mr. Darcy was condemned as the worst of men.

Chapter 11
Jane Goes to London

It was decided that Jane should get away from Longbourn for a few weeks. She was to stay in London with her uncle and aunt, Mr. and Mrs. Gardiner.

Secretly, Jane hoped to catch sight of Mr. Bingley—or at worst, his sister Caroline, while she was there. A week after her arrival, she wrote a letter to Elizabeth saying she had met Caroline.

Dearest Lizzie,

You were right. Miss Caroline Bingley has deceived me all along. She has no intention of letting me see Mr. Bingley. She came to the Gardiners's house today and it was clear she had no pleasure in doing so. She only stayed for a few moments and made a point of saying how Mr. Bingley was enjoying the company of Miss Darcy and that he did not intend to return to Netherfield ever again.

I cannot understand Mr. Bingley. His affections for me were once so strong. He must know I am in London. Surely Caroline Bingley would have told him. Yet he doesn't come to visit me. I can only think the worst.

I will write again when there is more news.

Your loving sister,
Jane

The letter made Elizabeth very sad. But at least the truth was out and Jane could not be duped by Caroline any more. "Let Mr. Bingley marry Darcy's sister," she said to herself. "He'll soon realize what he has thrown away in Jane."

The winter months passed slowly. Even Mr. Wickham seemed to have disappeared from the county. Not that Elizabeth was upset at that. Her feelings for him had cooled considerably.

In March, just a few months after Mr. Collins's marriage to Charlotte, Elizabeth decided that it was her duty, rather than a pleasure, to visit the pair in Hunsford.

She still thought of Mr. Collins as a pompous, narrow-minded, silly man. But, for Charlotte's sake, she would try and ignore the worst sides of his character.

The letter made Elizabeth very sad.

It was a long journey by carriage to Hunsford, just south of London. On the way, she visited Jane and the Gardiners in London. There she learned why Mr. Wickham had not been seen for some time. The scandalous gossip reported that he had eloped with a very plain but wealthy woman, called Mrs. King.

The news convinced Elizabeth that Mr. Wickham was not the honorable man he had first seemed, even though he had been poorly treated by Mr. Darcy.

The next day, Elizabeth left for Hunsford. The Reverend William Collins himself greeted her, when she arrived. "Honored! Honored! How honored we are to receive you in our humble abode," he said. "And that same welcome comes to you from my dear Lady Catherine de Bourgh, too."

Elizabeth's spirits sank. How could she bear to be in the same house as the foolish man?

Later Mr. Collins and Charlotte took Elizabeth on a tour of the gardens. Mr. Collins lost no time in pointing out Lady de Bourgh's mansion.

"Have you ever seen such a fine building?" he gushed. "And, of course, you will have the pleasure of meeting Lady de Bourgh tomorrow

"How honored we are to receive you."

after church. I'm sure she will honor you with some of her precious time."

"How kind of her," said Elizabeth, with a hidden smile.

"Lady de Bourgh is kindness itself," continued Mr. Collins. "Do you know that we actually dine with her twice a week? And we are never allowed to walk home. Her Ladyship's carriage is always provided for us. I should say one of Her Ladyship's carriages, for she has several."

They all returned to the Collins's modest cottage for lunch. They found that one of Lady de Bourgh's servants had left a note, inviting them all to dinner with her that very night.

Mr. Collins was quite overcome with gratitude. "I confess," he said, "that I should not have been surprised if Her Ladyship had asked us to take tea with her. But who could have imagined that we would be invited to dinner?"

Mr. Collins spent most of the afternoon telling Elizabeth what she might expect at dinner. He advised her not to be surprised at the great size of the rooms and the army of servants. He also hoped that the magnificence of the dinner didn't overpower her.

"And don't worry yourself," he advised, "if you haven't a fine dress for such a great occasion. Of course, Lady de Bourgh and her daughter, Miss de Bourgh, will be in their finest. But Her Ladyship won't expect you to be able to match her style. She would prefer you to be in a simple dress. She likes to see the differences in social rank preserved."

Mr. Collins, Charlotte, and Elizabeth walked through the gardens to Lady de Bourgh's home early that evening and were ushered into her presence by half a dozen liveried servants.

Mr. Collins was quite overcome.

Chapter 12
Dinner with Lady de Bourgh

"My Lady, how can we thank you for your generosity?" said Mr. Collins, bowing several times as he entered the dining room. Then he introduced Elizabeth.

Elizabeth soon discovered that Lady de Bourgh did not so much enjoy conversation. She took more enjoyment from lecturing people.

She inquired about Charlotte's domestic concerns and told her how to manage them. She explained how Charlotte should look after her cows and chickens. Lady de Bourgh didn't so much suggest anything. She gave orders about what should be done.

Then she turned her attention to Elizabeth. "Do you sing or play the piano?" she asked.

"A little," replied Elizabeth.

"Then we shall be happy to hear you at some time; though, I expect you will find our piano rather superior to what you are used to."

She turned her attention to Elizabeth.

Elizabeth was furious at the woman's rudeness.

"Do you draw?" asked Her Ladyship.

"No, not at all," replied Elizabeth.

"Oh dear," sighed Lady de Bourgh, "I suppose you were given no opportunity to learn. Your mother should have paid more attention to your education. Did you have a governess to teach you?"

"We never had a governess," said Elizabeth, quite sharply.

"No governess!" exclaimed Lady de Bourgh. "I never heard such a thing. Then who taught you as a child?"

"We never wanted for lack of an education," said Elizabeth, even more sharply than before. "I have, as you know, four sisters. Our parents taught us all well. We were never short of books."

"Nevertheless," said Her Ladyship, "I would have advised your mother to have had a governess. Only a governess can give a strict and correct education."

"I beg to differ in that opinion," said Elizabeth.

"Upon my word," said Lady de Bourgh, surprised that someone should disagree with her.

"You have strong opinions for one so young."

"I have been taught to speak as I believe," said Elizabeth.

Poor Mr. Collins was quite beside himself at Elizabeth's behavior. "Your Ladyship," he said, "I'm sure Elizabeth does not mean to be so bold."

Elizabeth replied without hesitation. "Dear Mr. Collins, I certainly do."

Lady de Bourgh almost choked on her food!

***

A few days later, Mr. Darcy arrived on a surprise visit to his aunt. He brought with him a cousin, Colonel Fitzwilliam.

Mr. Darcy was remarkably pleasant in his greetings to Elizabeth and asked how her family was. But she was only interested in one thing.

"Mr. Darcy," she said, "my elder sister Jane has been in London these last few weeks. Have you, by any chance, seen her?"

Elizabeth was keen to learn any news of what might have happened between Mr. Bingley and Jane. But Mr. Darcy said that he hadn't seen her at all.

Mr. Darcy was remarkably pleasant.

Elizabeth then asked about Mr. Bingley. "I have heard," she said, "that he has no intention of ever going back to Netherfield."

"I have never heard him say that," replied Mr. Darcy. "But he has a lot of friends in London and other places. So he probably won't be at Netherfield as much as he likes."

"And what brings you to Lady de Bourgh's on this occasion?" asked Elizabeth.

"To see my aunt, of course," said Mr. Darcy, looking rather uncomfortable.

Over the next few days Mr. Darcy called quite regularly at the Collins residence and, strangely, rarely visited his aunt.

Elizabeth was quite puzzled by his actions, but Charlotte was not. "My dear Lizzie," she confided to her friend one day, "he must be in love with you!"

Of course, Elizabeth laughed off the ridiculous idea.

While taking a walk in the gardens one afternoon, she met Colonel Fitzwilliam. Elizabeth took the chance to ask him about Mr. Darcy and Mr. Bingley. "They seem to a have a close friendship," she said.

"Oh, indeed," he replied. "I believe Mr. Darcy takes a lot of care of him. From what

Mr. Bingley tells me, he is greatly indebted to Mr. Darcy for saving him from entering a bad marriage. He advised Mr. Bingley to forget about his feelings for the woman."

Elizabeth guessed that the colonel was talking about Mr. Bingley and Jane. "Why did Mr. Darcy interfere in that relationship?" she asked, trying to hide her anger.

"I don't know the details," replied Colonel Fitzwilliam. "But I understand that the woman was unsuitable for Mr. Bingley."

Elizabeth was livid at hearing of her sister spoken off in such terms. But she still didn't reveal to the colonel that she knew who he was talking about.

"I think Mr. Darcy is just looking after Mr. Bingley's best interests," said Colonel Fitzwilliam. "Mr. Darcy distrusts some women. It might have something to do with a Mr. Wickham, who formed a friendship with Mr. Darcy's young sister, Georgiana."

When she returned to the Collins's house, Elizabeth went to her bedroom and burst into tears of anger. She was so furious she told Mr. Collins that she was not well enough to attend a second dinner that Lady de Bourgh had invited them to attend.

Trying to hide her anger.

Mr. Collins was beside himself. How could anyone be ill enough to refuse such a generous invitation from Lady de Bourgh?

Elizabeth only came downstairs again when everyone else had gone to dinner and she was alone. Some time later, the door bell rang. Elizabeth opened the door and to her utter amazement, Mr. Darcy walked into the room.

In a hurried manner, he said he had come to ask about her health and why she hadn't come to the dinner.

"I have a chill, I think," she answered him, as coldly as she could.

Mr. Darcy wouldn't sit down, but walked anxiously around the room in silence. Then, after a few minutes of silence, he came towards her.

"I have come to say something to you," he began. "I cannot hide my feelings any more. I have long admired you from afar. Indeed, I love you!"

Chapter 13
An Astonishing Proposal

Elizabeth was in total shock. She stared at Mr. Darcy in silence, not knowing how to reply.

He hadn't finished. "I know there is a difference of class between your family and mine. And common sense tells me I should fight these feelings. But I can't."

Elizabeth remained silent. She was thinking, and wasn't going to say anything until she had got over her surprise. But for every word he said, the angrier she was becoming. She could see that Mr. Darcy was confident that she would return his affection.

The color rose in her cheeks as she finally gave him a reply. "Mr. Darcy," she said, "I have never sought your love or affection. And I now find it very unfortunate indeed that you want to offer it to me. It is something I certainly do not want!"

As Elizabeth had foreseen, Mr. Darcy was astonished to be rebuffed. "So," he said at last,

"I have never sought your love."

"that is your uncivil answer. That is all I can expect, is it? You have rejected me? Well, I suppose it is of small matter."

"No!" replied Elizabeth. "That is not all. How could you be so outrageously cruel to tell me you love me when you are responsible for destroying my sister's happiness? Have you any idea how much I dislike you?"

Mr. Darcy's mouth dropped open. He did not understand what she meant.

"You cannot deny it!" continued Elizabeth furiously. "You cannot deny that you helped to destroy my sister Jane's relationship with Mr. Bingley. You alone turned him against her for no proper reason at all. Well? Can you deny it? My facts come from a very good source."

"I admit it," replied Mr. Darcy at last. "But I had my reasons and they were genuine and no cruelty was meant."

Elizabeth wasn't finished. "And there are other good reasons for my not liking you. Let's talk about Mr. Wickham. It was you and your family who reduced him to poverty. Your family owned so much, yet you deprived him of the income that should have been his. You are responsible."

"Oh yes," he replied, becoming angry

"You cannot deny it!"

himself, "his misfortunes have been great. And I thank you for pointing out that I was responsible. The truth is very different."

But Elizabeth was not listening any more. "There is nothing you can say which would make me change my attitude towards you. You have not behaved as a gentleman. You have behaved with conceit and selfishness. You are the last man in the world I would marry!"

"You have said quite enough!" snapped back Mr. Darcy. "I am sorry that I fell in love with you. I certainly wish it had never happened. Forgive me for taking up your precious time. Please accept my best wishes for your health and happiness in the future."

And with those words, he stormed out of the room and slammed the door behind him.

Elizabeth collapsed into a chair and burst into tears. She thought about the extraordinary events of the last few minutes, and shook her head.

Mr. Darcy in love with her! Mr. Darcy wanting to marry her! Marry her, despite destroying Jane's hopes of marrying Mr. Bingley!

It all seemed so incredible. His pride and arrogance seemed to know no bounds.

Chapter 14
Mr. Darcy's Letter

When Elizabeth woke the next morning, she was still in shock at what had happened the night before. After breakfast she went for a long walk in the gardens. She was on her way back to the Collins's house when she suddenly saw Mr. Darcy again.

Elizabeth turned away, hoping he had not seen her. But he called after her and soon caught up with her. He had a letter in his hand.

"Will you do me the honor of reading this?" he said, pushing the letter into her hand.

Then, with a slight bow, he turned and hurried away.

Elizabeth waited until he was out of sight and then opened it. She read it as she walked along the lane that led to the Collins's house.

Dear Miss Bennet,

Be not alarmed, I will not be making any new

Pushing the letter into her hand

proposals to you. You made it quite clear yesterday that you are not the least attracted to me. And I am writing without any intention of paining you, or humbling myself either. I just seek justice.

You accuse me of two offences. The first charge is that I destroyed any hopes of your sister Jane marrying Mr. Bingley. The second is that I have unfairly treated Mr. Wickham.

In my defense on the first matter, let me say this. During the dance at Netherfield, I saw how Mr. Bingley was falling in love with Jane. I have been a good friend of his for many years and I know all too well that he falls in love often. And all too often he has been rejected, at great pain to himself. So I watched your sister. She showed no signs of being in love with him. That was the reason why I persuaded him not to pursue her.

Now, if you tell me that in fact your sister had fallen in love with him, then I apologize for my error. Your anger was justified. I must also add in explanation that, for the same reason, I never told him when I discovered from Miss Caroline Bingley that Jane was in London staying with the Gardiners. That's why he didn't visit Jane.

So if I have hurt your sister's feelings, it was unknowingly done. It was only to protect Mr. Bingley. I must accept that it appears I have done something very wrong. And I must ask your forgiveness for it.

As for the second matter regarding Mr. Wickham, I will give you the plain facts. Mr. Wickham, as you probably know, is the son of the man who managed Pemberley Estate when my father was alive. He was an excellent man, much liked by my father. When Mr. Wickham was born my father became his godfather. He paid for his education and secured him a place at Cambridge University. There was nothing he didn't do to help that young man.

My father, on his deathbed, made me promise to support and help Mr. Wickham in any way I could. The only thing he added was that there was no need to give him any money because he had already left the man a fortune. Some time later, Mr. Wickham came to me and said he was in financial trouble. He appealed to me to give him some money in memory of the affection he and my father had enjoyed. I asked what had happened to the money my father had left him.

Promising to help Mr. Wickham.

He said he had never had a penny from my father.

It didn't take me long to confirm that a large sum had been left for him by my father. I also quickly found out that he had lost it all by gambling, drinking, and flirting with any number of women.

I told Mr. Wickham I knew the truth, but he refused to accept a word I said. The man is a cheat and a liar. Worse still, he even tried to elope with my sister Georgiana when she was just fifteen. Mr. Wickham's chief aim was clearly the girl's fortune!

I will have nothing to do with him. If you do not believe what I have said there are people, including Colonel Fitzwilliam, who can confirm everything I have told you.

I trust you will not dislike me even more by what I have told you in this letter. I shall not cause you any more annoyance. I leave for Pemberley at once.

I beg that you do not mention any of this to anyone. I loathe the man Wickham, but I won't demean myself by stooping to his level by making his treachery a matter of gossip for every Tom, Dick, and Harry. I would be grateful if you do not pass any of this information on to anybody else. I am leaving my trust in your hands.

Yours,
Fitzwilliam Darcy

Chapter 15
Pemberley

Elizabeth didn't know what to think. How could she believe the contents of the letter? She read it again; then twice more.

It slowly dawned on her that every word must be true. Colonel Fitzwilliam had already mentioned the matter of Mr. Wickham and Georgiana. She also remembered how Mr. Wickham had not come to the Netherfield ball, no doubt too frightened to face Mr. Darcy in public.

Suddenly, Elizabeth felt very ashamed. "How disgracefully I have behaved," she said to herself. "How could I have been so wrong? How could I have been so prejudiced against him?"

Elizabeth walked for a long time before she finally went back to the Collins's house. There she discovered that Mr. Darcy and Colonel Fitzwilliam had called to say goodbye. They were to travel to London on business and then move on to Pemberley.

A few days later it was time for Elizabeth to leave. It was now almost spring. Once more she stopped at the Gardiner's, in London. Jane was still there and Elizabeth revealed to her part of what she had learned from Mr. Darcy. She explained about Mr. Wickham's past.

The one matter that she did not mention was the fact that Darcy had admitted that he had persuaded Mr. Bingley to forget about Jane. Elizabeth was sure that Mr. Darcy would now make amends for that.

The carriage then took both Jane and Elizabeth home. When they reached Meryton, they were greeted by a familiar sight; their two younger sisters, Kitty and Lydia, dancing along the streets on the arms of two handsome army officers.

Both girls screamed with excitement when they saw the coach carrying Jane and Elizabeth. They ran to greet their sisters. They had no time to ask Jane and Elizabeth about their stay in London and Kent. All they wanted to talk about was the fact that the Meryton army regiment was moving to Brighton and how they wanted to spend the summer in Brighton.

Lydia had some interesting news about one particular army officer. "Have you heard

She stopped at the Gardiners', in London.

about Mr. Wickham?" she asked excitedly. "His relationship with Mary King is over. I knew he never cared for her. He only wanted her fortune. He cares for me more than he ever did her."

Elizabeth was acutely aware that the news only confirmed the type of behavior of which Mr. Darcy had accused Mr. Wickham. She would have warned Lydia about Mr. Wickham, but felt obliged by Mr. Darcy's letter not to reveal his true background. Hopefully Lydia had more sense than to get involved with Mr. Wickham.

Back at Longbourn at last, Mrs. Bennet immediately asked for news of Mr. Bingley. Elizabeth had decided that she wasn't going to tell her mother her news either. "I have heard no word from him," she said.

"He is a most undeserving man," complained Mrs. Bennet. "He will live to regret not marrying Jane. I shall not talk to him again, even if he does appear at Netherfield. And that seems most unlikely."

That summer, it was agreed that the younger girls could spend some time in Brighton. They were to stay with Colonel Forster, the commanding officer of the militia, and his wife.

They ran to greet their sisters.

Elizabeth had no intention of going to Brighton and by chance, meeting Mr. Wickham. A letter from the Gardiners gave her another option. They were going to travel north for a few weeks and tour the area. They invited Elizabeth to go with them.

The idea proved irresistible. Why, they might even visit Pemberley if Mr. Darcy was not in residence.

Elizabeth and the Gardiners were soon aboard a carriage rattling north. On the third night of their journey they found a comfortable inn to stay in, quite close to Pemberley. Elizabeth quickly discovered from the landlord that Mr. Darcy was still away.

The chance was too good to miss. The next day found them traveling down the long drive that led to Pemberley.

The park at Pemberley was vast, and covered with scores of beautiful trees. Sheep were grazing everywhere. For a while, Elizabeth saw no sign of the house. Then the drive began to climb. Suddenly, a magnificent mansion, rising up behind a huge lake, appeared before them.

Elizabeth had never seen a more beautiful or larger house in her life.

A magnificent mansion.

The carriage pulled up at the front of the house. Almost immediately the front door opened and a woman hurried out to greet them. It was Mrs. Reynolds, Mr. Darcy's house-keeper.

"And what can I do for you?" she asked.

The first thing that Elizabeth wanted to know was when Mr. Darcy was expected home.

"The day after tomorrow," explained Mrs. Reynolds.

Elizabeth then revealed to Mrs. Reynolds how they had met Mr. Darcy and asked if they could look around the estate.

Mrs. Reynolds was sure her master wouldn't object. In fact, she invited them in and took them on a tour of the building. "Mr. Darcy is so proud of his house," she said. "He is happy to let people see inside it when he is away."

One of the first rooms they saw was the nursery. "It's true what they say," observed Mrs. Reynolds. "A good-natured child will always grow up into a good-natured adult. And Mr. Darcy was always the most sweet-natured child."

"Is this the same Mr. Darcy I know?" wondered Elizabeth.

"He is also a fine master," continued Mrs.

Reynolds. "None better. There's no one around here who will give him a bad name, except that dreadful Mr. Wickham. He was a wrong-un and badly misused Mr. Darcy."

Mrs. Reynolds seemed a very wise and steady-minded woman to Elizabeth. So she was glad to hear confirmation about Mr. Wickham's bad nature.

"And Mr. Darcy is such a kind brother," said Mr. Reynolds as they passed through Georgiana's rooms. "There's nothing he wouldn't do for his sister."

Elizabeth was quite astounded to hear so many nice things said about a man whom she still thought of as rude and insulting. She found it hard to change her opinions of him despite what she was now learning about him.

After they had toured the mansion, Elizabeth and the Gardiners wandered off by themselves to explore the estate. Elizabeth was a short distance behind the Gardiners when she became aware of a rider approaching from the other side of the lake. She stopped and looked as the rider came closer, and then froze.

It was Mr. Darcy!

Chapter 16
A Surprise Meeting

Elizabeth and Mr. Darcy were just twenty yards apart. It was impossible for either to pretend they hadn't noticed the other. Mr. Darcy seemed the more surprised of the two and he brought his horse to a sudden halt.

Finally, he advanced again, dismounting once he'd reached Elizabeth. Their eyes met and both blushed. Elizabeth hastily looked away, trying to compose herself.

The Gardiners were also surprised. They stood some way off as Mr. Darcy started to talk to Elizabeth. Although they could not hear what he said, they saw the poor man's ever-increasing embarrassment.

In fact, Mr. Darcy was so embarrassed and surprised at the meeting that he could only mutter some meaningless comments about the weather.

"Oh, why did I come to Pemberley?" sighed Elizabeth, under her breath.

Yet, she had never seen Mr. Darcy so humble and polite.

The Gardiners approached and Elizabeth, finally pulling herself together, introduced them to Mr. Darcy. The man was politeness itself. He even told Mr. Gardiner to come and fish in Pemberley's lake whenever he was in the area.

"I have returned early," he said, "because I have to meet some visitors. Mr. Bingley and his sister are here tomorrow. My young sister Georgiana is due back here too. Miss Bennet, I would very much like you to meet her."

It was agreed that Mr. Darcy would bring her over to the inn at ten the next morning.

As arranged, a carriage arrived outside the inn on the following day. Inside were Mr. Darcy, Georgiana, and Mr. Bingley. Georgiana was just sixteen and taller than Elizabeth. She was a good-humored young lady and most polite and well-mannered. There was no pride or arrogance in her at all.

Georgiana was delighted to meet Elizabeth because, as she said, her brother had told her so much about her.

Elizabeth's meeting with Mr. Bingley also went well. She had completely forgiven the

Their eyes met and both blushed.

man. She knew that he was not to blame for hurting her sister Jane.

But Elizabeth dare not ask him the question she truly wanted an answer to: what were Mr. Bingley's true feelings for Jane? Did he really love Georgiana Darcy?

Mr. Bingley gave some hint of his feelings when he reminded Elizabeth that they hadn't met since November 26, the date of the dance at Netherfield. Elizabeth thought that to remember the exact date was very surprising. He also asked her how her sisters were, although he didn't mention Jane herself.

Elizabeth thought she saw some special tenderness in his eyes as he asked the question.

Mr. Darcy's party stayed for an hour.

"It's been so nice to see you again, Elizabeth," said Mr. Bingley. "No doubt we shall meet at Netherfield again this winter. We have lots of news to catch up on. I want to hear about all my Hertfordshire friends."

***

A letter to Elizabeth from Jane arrived at the inn the next morning. She went to her room and settled down to read it.

A good-humored young lady.

Dearest Lizzie,

Terrible news! We have just heard that our sister Lydia has run off with Mr. Wickham. She left Colonel Forster's house in Brighton without a word to anyone. This can only bring disgrace on our family.

Let us just hope that Mr. Wickham's character is not as bad as we hear it to be. But why would he want to marry Lydia? He must know that she has no money and is unlikely to receive any either.

Mother has retired to bed in shock and won't get out again. She says she will not leave her bed until she hears news that Lydia is home or properly married to the man. And Papa is just very angry at Lydia's irresponsibility.

Colonel Forster and Papa have now gone in search of the pair. They were last seen on the London road.

Dear Lizzie, if only we had warned her of what we knew about Mr. Wickham, none of this would have happened. You must return home as soon as possible.

Your loving sister,
Jane

As soon as she had read the letter, Elizabeth rushed downstairs to find Mr. and Mrs. Gardiner. She reached the bottom of the stairs and was astounded to find herself face-to-face with Mr. Darcy, who was just coming into the inn.

The letter had so shocked Elizabeth that her legs were trembling so much she could hardly stand.

She took one look at Mr. Darcy and burst into tears.

Terrible news!

Chapter 17
Disgrace Looms!

"It's Mr. Wickham!" Elizabeth sobbed. "He's run off with my sister, Lydia!"

Mr. Darcy took Elizabeth's arm and led her gently to a comfortable chair. "Now," he said, "be calm and tell me what has happened."

Between the falling tears, Elizabeth told him what was in the letter. "If only I had not kept the secret of Mr. Wickham to myself and Jane. I feel as if I am to blame for this disaster. The whole family will be disgraced. Oh, what a terrible mistake I have made!"

Mr. Darcy made no direct answer, but walked up and down the room looking very anxious. At last he spoke.

"Dear Elizabeth, I know you have long yearned to see me gone. You have made that quite clear. But I would do anything to help you and your family in this matter, especially as I am partly to blame because of my family's connection with Mr. Wickham."

"Tell me what has happened."

"There is one thing you can do," answered Elizabeth. "Keep my news a secret for as long as you can. If it gets out among the gossips, our family name will be disgraced more quickly than ever."

"You have my promise," he assured her before leaving.

After he had gone, Elizabeth thought it was very unlikely that she would ever see Mr. Darcy again. Their friendship or whatever it was, was so full of contradictions. She was beginning to wonder what she felt for him.

As she saw him board his carriage, she actually regretted that he was going out of her life. But her head was still too full of other emotions to know clearly what she thought about him.

Elizabeth went and found the Gardiners, who quickly agreed to return to Longbourn with her.

The journey home took two days. As soon as they arrived, Elizabeth ran up to her mother's bedroom.

"How could Lydia have done this?" cried Mrs. Bennet, on seeing her daughter. "And why did the Forsters ever let the girl out of their sight? They are to blame for this. Lydia is, after all,

Disgrace Looms!

"How could Lydia have done this?"

127

just sixteen. I always said the Forsters were unfit to look after her. What possessed the girl? They say Mr. Wickham has left huge debts all over Brighton and the rest of the country."

Mr. Gardiner entered the room and Mrs. Bennet became quite hysterical. "Brother dear," she cried, "you must join the hunt in London and seek her out. And if she is not married already, then make them marry! And if you find Mr. Wickham, don't let Mr. Bennet fight with him. For sure my husband will be killed if they do fight. And then what will happen to us? On Mr. Bennet's death, that dreadful Mr. Collins will turn us out of our house. Find them! Go now! And tell Mr. Bennet what a state I am in. I am frightened out of my wits. I have such terrible flutterings in every part of me; spasms in my sides, pains in my head, and such a beating in my heart."

Just then there was a knock at the front door. A letter had arrived. Elizabeth opened it. It was from Lydia and addressed to all the family.

To my dear family,

I know you will laugh when you get this letter and discover that I have gone. I am going to be

*married. And I'm sure you will never guess who
to. He is the one man in the world who I love. He
is an angel and I cannot be happy without him.
So when I see you next, don't forget that my new
name will be Mrs. Lydia Wickham. What a good
joke it will be! I can hardly write for laughing.*

> *Love to you all,*
> *Lydia*

Elizabeth and Jane both knew what a wild and
irresponsible girl Lydia could be. But to see
her elopement as a joke was too much.

"Oh thoughtless, thoughtless girl," sighed
Elizabeth.

But Mrs. Bennet was heartened by the
letter. "At least the man is to marry her," she
observed. "At least he is doing the honorable
thing. And what's more, at least one of my
daughters will be married at last!"

The next few days passed without any word
from Mr. Bennet, Colonel Forster, or Mr.
Gardiner, who had joined the search. Every
morning Mrs. Bennet called out to see if there
was any post. But the only letter that arrived
during that period was from the Reverend
William Collins to Mrs. Bennet.

"Oh, thoughtless, thoughtless girl."

Disgrace Looms!

Dear Mrs. Bennet,

I have just heard the news and feel obliged to write to give you my views and advice on the matter.

Be assured that Mrs. Collins and I sympathize with you all at a time when a respectable family such as yours is in so much distress. The death of young Lydia might have been a blessing in comparison to this disgrace, which we heard about through Lady de Bourgh.

Rest assured that she and I are completely in agreement on this matter. Her Ladyship says that Lydia's elopement will not help the fortunes of your other daughters who are still in need of a husband. Who will want to be connected to such a family now?

If Lydia is to marry Mr. Wickham, then so be it. But one hears that he has unpaid debts of many thousands of pounds. These are debts that can never be paid by either the man himself, or by your family.

Lady de Bourgh's—and my—advice to you would be to forget that Lydia was ever one of your family. Let her suffer that punishment for her dreadful offence.

Your loyal servant,
William Collins

Elizabeth was speechless at the cruelty and arrogance of the letter.

Two days later, Mr. Bennet returned home. He had given up the search for Lydia. "I will never let another army officer enter my house!" he shouted. "And all dancing and balls will be banned!"

Gloom settled over the Bennet house for the next few days. Then, at last, there was news of Lydia in a letter from Mr. Gardiner.

Chapter 18
News of Lydia

Mr. Gardiner's letter was addressed to Mr. Bennet, who read it out to his family.

"My dear Brother,

Soon after you left, a man came to see me with news of where Lydia and Mr. Wickham could be found in London. Please don't ask me who this man was. I am not free to reveal his name. But I went to see Lydia and Mr. Wickham. They are not married yet, but if family honor is to be upheld, it seems it would be best for them to do so. And Mr. Wickham is keen to marry her . . ."

At that moment Jane interrupted. "Mr. Wickham must be lying. He would not marry her unless someone had suddenly given Lydia a lot of money."

Mr. Bennet raised his hand and begged his

daughter to hear the entire letter. He continued reading.

"It now appears that all Mr. Wickham's debts have been paid. In addition, a yearly salary is also to be settled on both Lydia and Mr. Wickham. I am not yet in a position to explain where the money has come from, but rest assured it will provided.

Please let me know that you are happy with this arrangement and I will see to it that the wedding takes place . . ."

Mrs. Bennet shrieked with delight. "Oh, Mr. Bennet!" she exclaimed. "It is for the best! I shall have at least one daughter safely married, with an income to keep her. This is wonderful news. But who has produced the money? It must be Mr. Gardiner himself. He is such a generous man."

The wedding was duly arranged and took place in London soon after. None of the Bennet family attended the wedding, but a wedding party was arranged at Meryton a few days later.

Mr. Bennet refused to attend because he was still so angry at Lydia and Mr. Wickham's

Mrs. Bennet shrieked with delight.

elopement. But the rest of the family did go. They were all astounded at how happy Lydia appeared to be. She insisted on asking each member of the family to congratulate her on winning such a fine husband.

"I am sure all my sisters are envious of me finding such a kind and generous man for a husband," she laughed. "We are to live in the town of Newcastle and we shall have lots of balls. Of course, I shall make sure there are plenty of dancing partners for all my sisters."

Elizabeth and Jane could hardly bear it. They were relieved to see their sister so happy, yet they wondered if she would ever find out what a bad man Mr. Wickham truly was. How they prayed that Mr. Wickham would now change his ways.

It was during the party that Elizabeth discovered by accident that Mr. Darcy had attended Lydia's wedding in London. She was absolutely astounded at the news. Why should he have been there? After all, it was a hastily arranged marriage and Mr. Darcy was in no way connected by family to either Lydia or Mr. Wickham.

And, of course, Elizabeth knew the true story of how badly Mr. Wickham had used the Darcy

Elizabeth and Jane could hardly bear it.

family. What on earth had possessed him to go to the wedding? She quickly wrote a letter to Mrs. Gardiner, asking her if she had any idea why. A reply arrived a few days later.

My dear Elizabeth,

Mr. Darcy was indeed at the wedding. I think it is safe to say that he was there to make sure that the wedding took place and that Mr. Wickham not did leave Lydia waiting at the altar.

Dear Elizabeth, I have been keeping a secret from you. But now I see no harm in revealing it, although Mr. Darcy made it clear he did not wish it to become public knowledge.

Two days after we got home from our holiday in the north, Mr. Darcy called on us. First he told us that that he had found out where Lydia and Mr. Wickham were staying, and that he had spoken to them.

What he said exactly, I do not know. But he first insisted on Lydia leaving Mr. Wickham and returning to her family. Apparently she refused to do this. She was, she said, in love with Mr. Wickham and wanted to marry him. Mr. Darcy saw that there was to be no persuading her from the idea. So he made Mr. Wickham promise that he would do the honorable thing and marry her.

It was clear that Lydia loved Mr. Wickham far more than he would ever love her. But he agreed to the marriage, at Mr. Darcy's insistence.

It was also Mr. Darcy who paid off all Mr. Wickham's debts, arranged for a handsome wedding dowry to be given to Lydia, and secured an officer's rank in the army for Mr. Wickham. Mr. Darcy, in one leap, removed all the financial worries on the couple. Lydia will be well cared for financially.

Mr. Darcy was at the wedding.

You may ask why Mr. Darcy did all this. The truth is that he felt he was to blame for Lydia running off with Mr. Wickham. He felt that as Mr. Wickham had once been connected to his own family, then it was his job to remedy any disgrace caused by the man. He felt he must help our family in that difficult time by doing anything he could . . .

Elizabeth put down the letter. She was absolutely astonished at what she had learned from it. Her heart was pounding with emotion.

She found it rather painful to discover that the man whose marriage proposal she had so rudely and brutally turned down, was the man now responsible for restoring Lydia's honor and helping Mr. Wickham—a man whom he had no love for at all.

Elizabeth felt very humbled. She realized now how prejudiced she had been toward the so-proud Mr. Darcy.

The next day there was more news. Mr. Bingley and his family were about to return to Netherfield for a long stay.

Chapter 19
Mr. Bingley Returns

Mrs. Bennet was all a-twitter once more at the news of Mr. Bingley returning. "Yes, Jane, I know I said I would never speak to him again," she laughed. "But perhaps it's best for you to pay him every attention when he comes. He might make a husband yet."

Jane, of course, was still unaware of the circumstances that had left Mr. Bingley thinking she had no interest in him. Elizabeth had still not told her. Elizabeth was still convinced that if Mr. Bingley truly loved her sister, he would soon show it.

Jane herself pretended she had lost interest in the man. But that was not the truth of the matter. She still adored him.

An invitation to dine at Longbourn was sent to Netherfield as soon as Mr. Bingley arrived. An acceptance quickly followed. Mr. Bingley said he would love to come but added that his sister Caroline was unavailable.

On the afternoon of the dinner, the ladies of Longbourn were all at an upstairs window, waiting for their guest to arrive. Kitty spotted Mr. Bingley riding toward the house first.

"Mamma, Mr. Bingley's coming," she cried excitedly, looking out of the window. "And there's another gentleman with him."

Mrs. Bennet looked out. "Good gracious! It's Mr. Darcy. I hate the sight of him. He's the one who was so rude to my dear Elizabeth. But never mind that; any friend of Mr. Bingley's will always be welcome here, I suppose."

Elizabeth had also rushed to the window to see the arrival of Mr. Darcy. She had decided that she would not pay any special attention to him, but just watch and see how he behaved.

She was more interested in seeing how Mr. Bingley would treat Jane. She was not disappointed. At dinner, he sat down beside Jane and the two never stopped talking and laughing together all evening. Elizabeth was delighted. She could see a marriage proposal on the horizon. She had been right all along about Mr. Bingley's feelings for Jane.

Mr. Darcy was sitting at the opposite end of the table to Elizabeth. He said little, even to those closest to him. He occasionally

"Good gracious! It's Mr. Darcy."

exchanged glances with Elizabeth.

How Elizabeth's views on Mr. Darcy had changed! She now saw a very different man to the one she first met. The new Mr. Darcy was handsome, honorable, and generous.

But why should he pay her any attention now? She had rejected his proposal of marriage so brutally.

"Why should I be so foolish to imagine that he would ask me a second time?" she asked herself.

***

The following day, Mr. Bingley arrived at Longbourn by himself. He had come to see Mr. Bennet for a private talk. The two shut themselves away in his study. A few minutes later, a smiling Mr. Bingley emerged and Mr. Bennet asked Jane to join him in the study.

"Well I never," said the kindly Mr. Bennet. "I have lost my wildest daughter to Mr. Wickham and now the most eligible Netherfield bachelor has asked my permission to marry you."

"What did you say?" cried Jane.

"Of course, I said I would be delighted."

Jane hugged her father in delight. She gave

Hugging her father in delight.

him a huge kiss and then ran out to kiss her husband-to-be. Suddenly, the house was in an uproar of excitement.

Mrs. Bennet was quite hysterical with joy. "Oh, it's too much!" she cried. "A wealthy gentleman for my Jane. Oh, I won't sleep a wink tonight. I'm far too happy. Oh what a handsome man he is! How could I have ever thought badly of him?"

When the news of the engagement reached the other neighboring families in the area, there was more excitement.

The Bennets were now thought to be the luckiest family around. What a catch Mr. Bingley had been!

Chapter 20
A Surprise Visitor

A week after Jane's engagement to Mr. Bingley, there was a surprise visitor to Longbourn. It was Lady Catherine de Bourgh and she was in a very angry mood indeed.

She took Elizabeth into the garden for a private conversation. "I am not to be trifled with," she began. "A report of the most alarming nature has reached me. I was told that not only is your sister Jane engaged, but that in all likelihood there would soon be an engagement between yourself and my nephew, Mr. Darcy! I know it must be a scandalous falsehood. It cannot possibly be true."

"If you know it can't be true," replied Elizabeth boldly, "then why have you traveled all this way to say how angry you are?"

"I want to hear you deny it," snapped Her Ladyship.

"Your ladyship has already declared it impossible," answered Elizabeth, trying to

Lady de Bourgh was in a very angry mood.

puzzle out where such a rumor had come from.

"Don't play games with me!" snorted Lady de Bourgh. "If it is true, let me tell you that it can never happen. He is promised to my daughter already. They have been intended for each other since they were children."

"If that is the case, then you have no reason to worry," continued Elizabeth.

The more Elizabeth stood her ground, the angrier Lady de Bourgh became. "Tell me at once," she stormed, "are you or are you not engaged to Mr. Darcy?"

"It is nothing to do with you, madam," replied Elizabeth. "But to send you away happier than you came, I can confirm that I am not engaged to him as of now."

"And will you promise never to enter into such an engagement?" she boomed in answer.

"I will make no promise of the kind," replied Elizabeth sharply.

Lady de Bourgh was shaking with anger. "Miss Bennet," she said, "I am shocked and astonished. I thought you were a reasonable woman. I shall not leave until you have given me a promise."

"You will have to wait a long time," said

Elizabeth calmly. "I am not frightened of your words. I don't know how much you can interfere in the life of your nephew, but you certainly have no right to meddle in mine!"

"Don't be so hasty, girl!" said Her Ladyship. "I need not add that I know everything about your sister Lydia's infamous elopement, and her being saved from disgrace by a marriage to a complete rogue. Pemberley was once polluted by the presence of Mr. Wickham. Now is it to be polluted again by you moving in as mistress of the house?"

That was the final insult. "Lady Catherine," said Elizabeth, "I have nothing farther to say to you."

"Then you are determined to have my nephew as your husband?" she asked. "A man of such higher social class and honor? You would disgrace him by marrying him?"

"I repeat, we are not engaged," said Elizabeth. "But if he should ever ask for my hand in marriage, then I would not hesitate in accepting him."

With that, she put her head proudly in the air, turned, and walked into the house.

Her family was quite astonished at the arrival of Lady de Bourgh and were equally surprised when Her Ladyship boarded her carriage and cried out to the driver, "Home, coachman! I will not stay a minute longer in this dreadful place!"

Neither Mrs. Bennet, nor anyone else in the family, could get Elizabeth to explain what it had all been about. Elizabeth herself was completely confused, too. Mr. Darcy had not asked her to marry him again. So was there any truth in the rumors that Lady de Bourgh had heard?

Two days later, Mr. Bennet called Elizabeth into his study. He had a wry smile on his face. "I have received a letter that has astonished me exceedingly," he said. "To be sure, I was not aware that I had two of my daughters on the brink of marriage. Let me congratulate you on a very fine conquest."

Elizabeth knew of nothing that had happened to make her father so convinced she was to marry. Perhaps the letter was from Lady de Bourgh or Mr. Darcy. She was wrong on both counts. It was from the Reverend William Collins and Mr. Bennet read it out.

Dear Mr. Bennet,

I am to congratulate you on the engagement

"Home, coachman!"

announced between your daughter Jane and Mr. Bingley. Yet, I now hear that Elizabeth is to marry Mr. Darcy, perhaps the most eligible bachelor in the land.

I would caution you on this matter. You might feel it right to discourage your daughter from such a marriage. I have reason to believe that Lady de Bourgh is very much against such a marriage.

Indeed, she has told me that she will not give her consent to the marriage. I thought it my duty to tell you that it would be foolhardy to enter a marriage without her gracious permission, a permission that I am reliably informed she will never give.

Your cousin,
Rev. William Collins.

Mr. Bennet put down the letter. "Now this is very strange," he said. "I thought you hated this man Mr. Darcy; a man who cruelly insulted you at Netherfield only last year."

There was now a knowing smile on Mr. Bennet's face. "Was that the reason we were honored with a visit from Lady de Bourgh two days ago?" he asked. "Did she come personally to prevent any such engagement and marriage?"

Elizabeth began to laugh. She told her father all of what had happened in the last few months. "So you see," she said, "I am as much confused about all this as you. As far as I am concerned, he has not proposed to me a second time and has no intention of doing so. So you can tell dear Mother that she can't get rid of yet another daughter quite yet!"

"Let me congratulate you."

Chapter 21

A Walk in the Country

Mr. Darcy and Mr. Bingley arrived together at Longbourn the very next day.

"It's such a nice day," said Mr. Bingley. "We are in need of a good walk."

So it was that Mr. Bingley, with Jane on his arm and Mr. Darcy, with Elizabeth beside him, walked off into the country.

Gradually, so very gradually, the two couples became separated. Mr. Bingley and Jane were now walking well ahead of the other two. Elizabeth could contain herself no more. One way or the other, she had to find out what was going on in Mr. Darcy's mind.

"Mr. Darcy," she said, "I must thank you for what you did in the matter of my sister Lydia and Mr. Wickham. You saved my family's good name."

"It was meant to be a secret," he replied. "I never intended that you should find out about that. But I must confess that I did it for you, rather than your family."

Mr. Darcy hesitated before he continued talking. "The truth is," he said, "my affection for you has not changed. But if your feelings toward me are the same as they were when we last spoke of this matter, then please tell me now and I will never trouble you again."

Elizabeth knew she had to open her heart to Mr. Darcy now or lose him forever.

"I think you know already," she said, "that my feelings have changed a great deal toward you. I am not as prejudiced as I was before."

"And neither am I so proud as to take your affection for granted," he replied.

They walked on in silence. A little farther on, a smile crossed Mr. Darcy's face. "I did guess," he confessed, "that perhaps my hopes were not in vain."

"But how?" asked Elizabeth.

"By the fact that you told my aunt you would never promise *not* to marry me!" he replied.

Now it was Elizabeth's turn to smile. He had obviously heard of the angry meeting between her and Lady de Bourgh. "And where did Lady de Bourgh hear those rumors about an engagement between you and I?"

Mr. Darcy admitted that he had teased

Opening her heart to Mr. Darcy.

his aunt by suggesting he might one day win Elizabeth's heart.

Then the conversation began to flow. First, Mr. Darcy begged forgiveness for what he had said when they first met at the Netherfield Ball. "I shall never forget how you said I might have behaved in a more gentlemanly manner. Your words have echoed guiltily in my head ever since."

Then it was Elizabeth's turn. "And I apologize for being so rude to you at Lady de Bourgh's. And when I read your letter, it was the beginning of the end for many of my prejudices against you."

"Oh, I still have to mend some of my ways," Mr. Darcy continued, taking her hand. "I have been selfish all my life. As a child I was taught right and wrong. But I failed to learn lessons about controlling my pride. I am an only son and became very spoilt. It was you, dearest Elizabeth, who taught me the real lessons in life. I would like to talk to Mr. Bennet about it this evening if I might."

Elizabeth realized that he was talking about an engagement. But any further thoughts were stopped as Jane and Mr. Bingley shouted back to them to hurry up.

Talking about an engagement.

"We'll be late home for tea," cried Jane.

That night Elizabeth opened her heart to Jane. "I think we are engaged," she said.

"What!" gasped Jane. "To Mr. Darcy? You're joking. This cannot be! You dislike him so much. In fact, you hate him."

Elizabeth explained everything that had happened since spending time with the Collins's at Lady de Bourgh's.

"I speak nothing but the truth," said Elizabeth. "I love him. He loves me. And we are engaged if Papa approves it."

"Good heavens!" cried Jane. "Now I must believe it. You have my congratulations."

"So you will like having him as a brother?" asked Elizabeth.

"Very, very much," answered Jane. "Nothing could give Mr. Bingley and I more delight."

Jane and Elizabeth talked the night away, and watched excitedly as Mr. Darcy arrived the next day. He proceeded straight to Mr. Bennet's study.

Half an hour later, Mr. Darcy emerged with a smile on his face. "Your father would like to see you," he said quietly.

Chapter 22
Mr. Darcy and Elizabeth

"I am still confused," said the long-suffering Mr. Bennet as his favorite daughter sat down in his study. "You want to marry Mr. Darcy and yet we all thought you hated him. Is it because he is rich? That he will buy you expensive clothes and run you around in great carriages?"

"You know me better than that, Papa," Elizabeth replied. "Yes, I did hate him and it is only recently that I have discovered the real Mr. Darcy. I have fallen in love with him and he with me. We have forgiven each other for the rudeness of the past."

"Well that is good to hear," said Mr. Bennet, "because I have given him my permission to marry you. Mr. Darcy is the kind of man, indeed, who I should never dare refuse anything."

It was then that Elizabeth revealed what Mr. Darcy had done for the family in relation to Lydia. Mr. Bennet listened with astonishment.

"What!" he said at last when Elizabeth finished speaking. "Mr. Darcy made the match between Wickham and Lydia? Gave them money? Paid the fellow's debts? Got him a place as an officer in the army?"

"Everything," replied Elizabeth.

"In that case," said Mr. Bennet, "I could not have parted with you for someone more worthy that Mr. Darcy. He will be a wonderful husband if he treats you as well as he has treated this family."

Elizabeth threw herself into Mr. Bennet's arms and gave him a huge kiss.

"Does Mrs. Bennet know of this yet?" he asked when he had finally escaped from the arms of his adoring daughter.

"No," said Elizabeth. "I shall go and see her now."

"Treat her gently," laughed Mr. Bennet. "The shock of it all might put her into an attack of hysterics, the likes of which we've never seen before."

He was right.

"Good gracious, girl!" she screamed on hearing Elizabeth's news. "Lord bless me! Dear me! Mr. Darcy! Who would have thought it! Is it really true? Oh my dear Elizabeth, think how

"He will be a wonderful husband."

rich you will be. What carriages you will have! What clothes! Why Jane will think herself a pauper compared to you! Such a handsome man! So tall! I must apologize if you thought I once hated him. I hope he will overlook that. Dear, dear Lizzie! A house in the country and another in town."

Mrs. Bennet had to sit down to get her thoughts together. "Oh, Lizzie. Now I have three daughters married or about to be married. All rich. All happily settled. What a strange place this world is. Who knows, by next Saturday I wouldn't be surprised now to hear that Kitty and Mary have found husbands too."

Meanwhile, in his study, Mr. Bennet was writing a letter.

Dear Mr. Collins,

I thank you for your recent letter. Yes, Elizabeth will soon be the wife of Mr. Darcy. You may try and console Lady de Bourgh as well as you can. But if I were you, I would take the side of Mr. Darcy in this.

And should you persist in seeking to move into this house when I die, please don't let that worry you any more. I am sure that Elizabeth

"Good gracious, girl!"

and Mr. Darcy will provide a comfortable home for those who survive me, at Pemberley.

Yours sincerely,
Mr. Bennet

Mr. Darcy had also written a letter to his aunt.

Mr. Bennet was writing a letter.

Mr. Darcy and Elizabeth

Your Ladyship,

I wish to inform you that Elizabeth Bennet has made me the happiest of men by agreeing to marry me. I sincerely hope that you never try to bully her again. As you discovered, Elizabeth Bennet is made of stronger stuff. She is not a lady to be bullied.

Yours sincerely,
Fitzwilliam Darcy

Chapter 23
The Story Ends

Jane and Mr. Bingley, and Elizabeth and Mr. Darcy were married on the same day in the same church at Longbourn. Neither Lady de Bourgh, Caroline Bingley, nor Mr. Collins attended.

Soon after their wedding, Elizabeth and Mr. Darcy moved into Pemberley. Not long after that, Mr. Bingley bought an estate nearby. Elizabeth and Jane were delighted to find themselves close neighbors.

Mrs. Bennet, having got rid of three of her daughters in marriage, now missed them very much. Fortunately, she still had Mary and Kitty at home. Mr. Bennet sorely missed Elizabeth, his favorite.

So Mr. and Mrs. Bennet regularly traveled north to enjoy the comforts of Pemberley. How Lady de Bourgh glared at the "pollution" visiting the estate so often.

Caroline Bingley had cut herself off from her brother and Mr. Darcy since the wedding.

The Story Ends

They were married on the same day.

But she grew to regret her decision. She had always loved to be seen in wealthy society at Pemberley. So she gradually wheedled her way back into Mr. Darcy and Elizabeth's social circle.

She was soon heard boasting how friendly she was with the new mistress of Pemberley. But Elizabeth never quite trusted her. In turn, Caroline never forgave Jane for destroying any hopes of a marriage between Mr. Bingley and Georgiana Darcy, nor Elizabeth herself for stealing Mr. Darcy from under her own nose.

Lydia Bennet grew older but never wiser. She hadn't come to the weddings, but did send Elizabeth a note of congratulation.

Dear Lizzie,

I wish you great joy. If you love Mr. Darcy half as much as I love Mr. Wickham, you must be very happy. It is a great comfort to me to know that you are now so rich. And when you have nothing better to do, I hope you will think of us. I don't think we shall have quite enough money to live on without some help. A few hundred pounds a year would be very useful.

Your loving sister,
Lydia

The Story Ends

The Bennets regularly visited Pemberley.

Elizabeth was determined never to spoil her sister with any money. But of course, her generosity prevented it. She regularly sent money to her wayward and spendthrift sister who was forever getting into debt, along with her husband.

Lady de Bourgh remained furious about Elizabeth and Mr. Darcy's wedding for many years after. In her older years, she regularly sent rude letters to the couple, still complaining that they had married without her permission.

Mr. Collins never visited. He was too much in fear of his mistress, Lady de Bourgh. But his wife Charlotte, Elizabeth's best friend, did travel north at times.

The Gardiners visited Pemberley often and were on the best of terms with Elizabeth and Mr. Darcy. It was, after all, they who first took Elizabeth to Pemberley; a day marked by Mr. Darcy's sudden and surprise appearance. It was only after that meeting that Elizabeth and her prejudice began to learn to love the proud Mr. Darcy.

Elizabeth and Mr. Darcy were forever grateful that the Gardiners helped bring them together.

The End